The EXPERIMENTS of DOCTOR VERMIN

Written and Illustrated by TIM EGAN

HOUGHTON MIFFLIN COMPANY
BOSTON 2002

For our two brave sons,
Chris and Brian

www.houghtonmifflinbooks.com

The text of this book is set in Trump Mediaeval.
The illustrations are ink and watercolor on paper.

Library of Congress Cataloging-in-Publication Data

Egan, Tim.
The experiments of Doctor Vermin / by Tim Egan.
p.   cm.
Summary: Sheldon, a pig who works as a short-order cook, encounters a mad scientist
one stormy Halloween night and must face all of his biggest fears.
ISBN 0-618-13224-4
[1. Fear—Fiction. 2. Pigs—Fiction. 3. Wolves—Fiction. 4. Science—Experiments—Fiction.
5. Halloween—Fiction. 6. Cooks—Fiction.] I. Title.
PZ7.E2815 Ex 2002
[Fic]—dc21   2001039630

Manufactured in the United States of America
PHX 10 9 8 7 6 5 4 3 2 1

SHELDON HAD NEVER CARED MUCH FOR HALLOWEEN. In fact, aside from wolves and thunderstorms, he was probably more frightened of that particular night than of just about anything.

He was a short-order cook by trade, and this Halloween he was out looking for work when his car broke down. At precisely that moment, thunder crackled overhead and it started to rain. Worst of all, Sheldon could hear wolves howling in the nearby forest. Needless to say, the poor little pig was absolutely terrified.

As he sat trembling in his car, lightning lit up a mansion on the hill above him. Though it looked scary, he felt he had little choice but to go and ask for help, so he ran up the steps and knocked on the giant front doors.

"Hello!" he shouted. "Is anybody home?"

There was no answer, so he knocked again. Suddenly, the step underneath him opened up and he fell into a dark tunnel. He didn't even have time to scream.

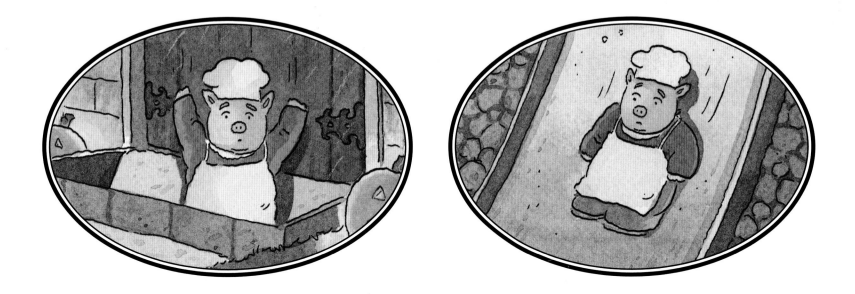

He landed on a hard surface, and before he could catch his breath, lights flashed on and a crazy-looking man ran over, strapped him down, and said, "A pig, eh? I suppose that will have to do."

Sheldon started sputtering, "Hello . . . uh . . . I'm Sheldon . . . I'm a cook . . ."

"*Silence!*" shrieked the man. "You will be my finest achievement! With you as my monster, I, Doctor Edmund Vermin, shall rule the world! Ah ha ha haaa!" The man flipped the switch, and words couldn't describe the terror Sheldon felt at that moment.

He closed his eyes as tight as he could. There was a loud explosion and a blinding flash of light. Then his entire body started to grow. When he opened his eyes, he looked down to see that he had turned into a pig four times his normal size.

The doctor was thrilled with the results.
"It worked!" he squealed. "You're huge, and I'm in complete control of your mind!"
But this was where the evil doctor was wrong.

Although it was true that Sheldon was gigantic, his mind was still his own. He knew he was still Sheldon, the short-order pig. He decided to play along so that the evil doctor wouldn't get angry.

"Follow me," commanded the doctor.

"Yes, Master," said Sheldon as he followed him up the stairs, trying to look as if he

were under the doctor's spell. They walked into a large kitchen, and Doctor Vermin reached into the refrigerator and pulled out a liverwurst sandwich. Sheldon had a strong dislike for liverwurst. He had always felt it had an appropriate name.

The doctor held out the sandwich and said, "Here, eat this."

"No, thanks," said Sheldon. "I'm not really hungry."

"Curses!" shouted the doctor. "I knew you were faking! You're not under my spell at all! You're of no use to me! Get out, pig monster!"

In a total panic, Sheldon ran down the dark hallway and out into the storm.

Above the rain, he heard wolves, and even though he was now much larger, he still didn't feel any safer. The howling sent shivers up and down his enormous spine. He saw another mansion in the woods, so he ran and pounded on the door.

"Somebody help me!" he shouted.

A pleasant-looking lady in a queen's costume opened the door and said, "Oh, how delightful. A giant pig chef. Trick or treat." She handed Sheldon a candied apple and began closing the door.

"No!" yelled Sheldon. "You don't understand! I'm a normal pig! My name is Sheldon! A mad scientist turned me into a giant!" The woman dropped her tray of apples.

A man ran into the parlor. "Margaret!" he said. "What is it?"

"This pig claims that he was transformed into a giant by a mad scientist," she said.

The man dropped his tray of apples as well.

"It can't be," he said. "Doctor Vermin was taken to an insane asylum three years ago."

If Sheldon had been holding a tray of apples, he definitely would have dropped it.

"You mean you know him?" Sheldon asked in disbelief.

"We know him, all right," said the man. "I'm Harry, by the way, and this is my wife, Margaret. Three years ago, Doctor Vermin lured us into his laboratory and tried to turn us into giants so he could rule the world."

"It was dreadful," said Margaret, "but the experiment failed and he let us go. We called the police and they arrested him. Months later, Simon Banning moved in and he's been there ever since, so I don't see how . . . "

"There's a madman living there," interrupted Sheldon. "I'll prove it."

The three headed off into the woods.

"So the experiment had no effect on you?" asked Sheldon.

"Not true," said Harry. "He turned us into humans."

"What were you before?" asked Sheldon.

"Wolves," they answered together.

Sheldon jumped back, but since Harry and Margaret weren't wolves anymore, it seemed silly to feel afraid of them.

"It must have been great to be fearless," he said. "I've always envied wolves for that."

Margaret laughed and said, "Oh, Sheldon, we were afraid of things, just like I'm scared right now."

"Indeed," said Harry. "I've always been a bit jittery in the dark myself."

They reached the mansion, and Sheldon made sure that none of them stood on the steps. He knocked loudly and yelled, "Trick or treat!"

The porch light turned on, and a mouse opened the door and said, "Harry. Margaret. Happy Halloween. I see you've brought a friend. Here you go, pig giant."

He held out a piece of candy.

"Wait a minute!" said Sheldon. "Where's Doctor Vermin?"
"Why, I haven't heard that name in years!" said the mouse.
"Nor had we, Simon," said Margaret, "but this pig claims the doctor is here."
The mouse shivered and said, "Just the thought chills me to the bone."

"I'm not making this up!" Sheldon insisted as he ran over to the laboratory door. "Down there!" he yelled. "That's where it happened!"

He raced down the stairs as Harry, Margaret, and Simon followed him. Sheldon switched on the lights and said, "What do you call this?"

"I call it the library," said Simon. "Now will you please leave?"
To Sheldon's dismay, they were standing in a spectacular room filled with books.
"It's exquisite," noted Margaret.
"Indeed," said Harry. "Quite impressive. Awfully sorry about all this, Banning."

"This is insane!" cried Sheldon. "This was like a dungeon!"

He banged his head against the wall, which started rumbling. In an instant, they all whirled around into the sinister laboratory of Doctor Vermin.

"I told you!" shouted Sheldon. "Doctor Vermin is here!"

"It's true, you fools!" shrieked the mouse. "I was tired of being a tiny rodent, so years ago I attempted to become gigantic, but I turned myself into a man by accident. In the asylum I discovered something that reverses the process. I changed back into a mouse and escaped with ease! And now, I can turn into either Simon or the brilliant Doctor Vermin at will!"

He took a swallow from a test tube and turned back into the evil doctor.

Harry and Margaret screamed, but Sheldon, without hesitating, jumped and landed on the doctor. Margaret quickly ran upstairs and called the police, who came and took Doctor Vermin back to the asylum, where they promised he would never escape again.

After he was gone, Sheldon picked up the test tube and said, "I don't know about you two, but I want to be myself again."

He was about to drink from it when Harry yelled, "Sheldon, wait! We don't know what's in there."

Sheldon decided it was worth the risk. He took a sip and said, "It tastes like horse-radish."

A moment later, he turned back into regular old Sheldon. He then handed the test tube to Margaret, who after tasting it turned back into a beautiful wolf.

"Margaret!" exclaimed Harry. "You look simply ravishing!"

Harry then tasted it and turned back into a wolf himself.

"Oh, how I've missed that lovable snout of yours," said Margaret.

"You know," said Sheldon, "I actually feel more comfortable as a timid little pig."

"Timid?" said Harry. "You must be joking. Your car broke down on a stormy Halloween night and you ran up to a dark mansion. After being turned into a giant, you insisted on coming back. You exposed the secret of Doctor Vermin and then captured him yourself. You tested the secret formula, and seeing that it worked, you gave it to us, knowing full well that we're wolves. The way I see it, you must be the bravest pig in the world."

It was something that Sheldon had never even considered.

As they walked out into the night, Margaret said, "You know, Sheldon, we could use a cook and we've got plenty of room. Would you consider staying with us?"

"Indeed!" said Harry. "Just promise not to use horseradish!"

Sheldon accepted, and they all shared a good laugh on what turned out to be the best, if not strangest, Halloween that Sheldon had ever had.